A Birthday Wish

FROZEN903576

Code is valid for your Disney Frozen ebook and may be redeemed through the Disney Story Central app on the App Store. Content subject to availability. Parent permission required. Code expires on December 31, 2019.

Bath • New York • Cologne • Melbourne • Delhi
Hong Kong • Shenzhen • Singapore

Little Brothers

Olaf loves his little brothers! Count the snowgies, then color in this sweet picture of them ice-skating.

There are ☐☐ snowgies

Answer on page 31

Birthday Search

Anna is super excited for her birthday celebrations!
Can you find the fun words in the grid below?
Look up, down, across, and diagonally.

BALLOON

PARTY

HAPPY

CAKE

GIFT

B	P	O	N	F	T	I	F
Y	B	A	L	L	O	O	N
P	I	Y	R	N	P	I	H
P	H	C	B	T	H	O	N
A	I	A	O	C	Y	N	B
H	C	K	I	Y	O	B	P
O	P	E	C	G	I	F	T

Answers on page 31

Super searching!

3

Cute Cake

Copy Anna's beautiful birthday cake into the empty grid below, drawing one square at a time. Then color it in!

Way to go!

Add your reward sticker here.

4

Anna's Banner

The snowgies have knocked down Anna's birthday banner! Help Sven put the last three letters in the right place.

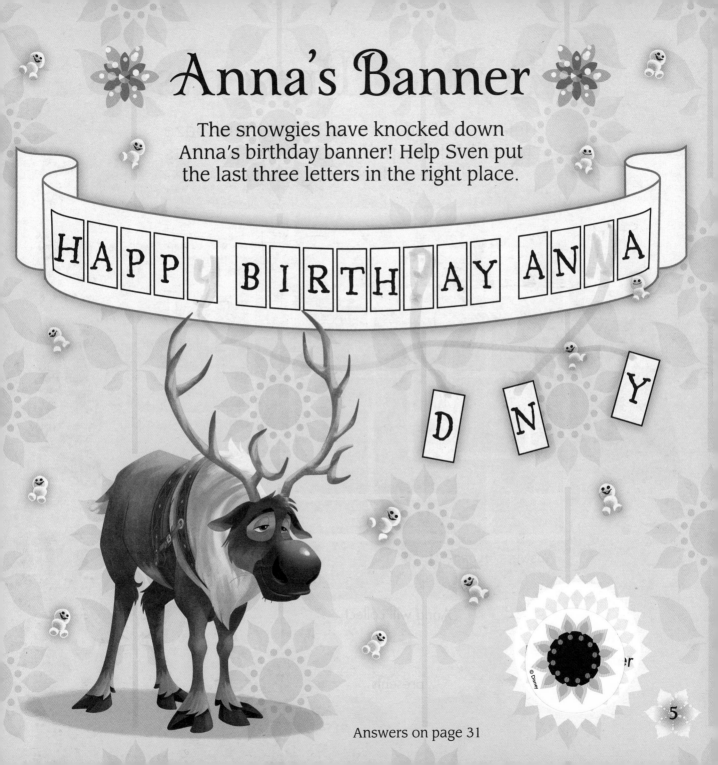

HAPP Y BIRTH AY AN A

D N Y

Answers on page 31

5

Perfect Presents

Help Anna find her way through the maze to her birthday party. How many presents will she collect along the way?

Start

Finish

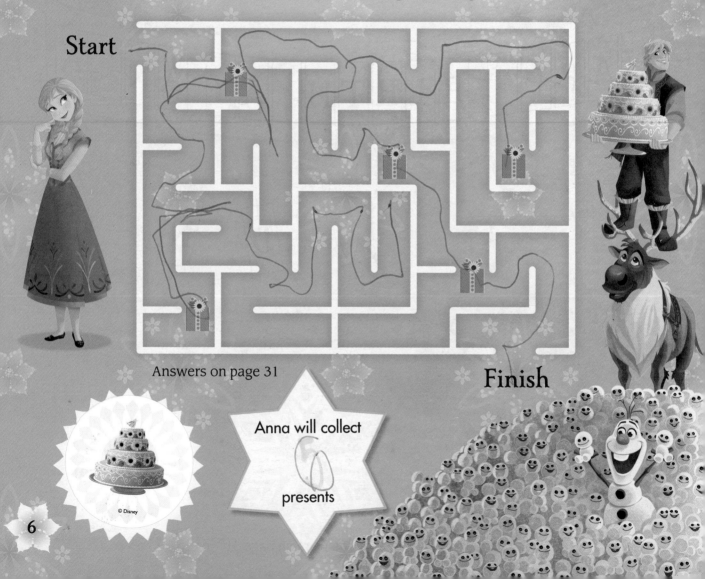

Answers on page 31

Anna will collect

6

presents

6

Glam Gown

How many sunflowers can you see on Anna's new dress? Write your answer in the space below, then color her in!

There are
6
sunflowers

Answer on page 31

7

Uh-oh, Olaf!

Olaf just can't help having a bite of
Anna's tasty ice cream cake!
Color in this picture of him and Elsa.

Perfect!

Add your
reward sticker
here.

Rise and Shine!

It's time for Elsa to wake Anna up.
Use the key below to help Elsa find
her way to Anna's bedroom.

Start ←

↓
Finish

Key

↑	↓	←	→

Answer on page 31

Balloon Race

Anna's birthday present is attached to one of these balloons. Help her find the right balloon before her gift floats away!

A

B

C

You did it!

© Disney

Answer on page 31

Which Snowgie?

One of these snowgies is different from the others. Can you spot him?

A

B

C

D

E

Did you find him?

Answer on page 31

11

Family Portrait

One of Anna's birthday presents is a special family portrait. Can you draw a picture of your family in the frame below?

Dot-to-Dot Dress

Elsa has made a dazzling dress with her icy magic. Help her finish it by connecting the dots and coloring it in.

Magical!

Celebration Cakes

There are lots of delicious cakes ready for Anna's party.
Spot and circle the only cake that isn't
part of a matching pair.

A

B

C

D

E

F

G

14

Answer on page 31

© Disney

No Time to Lose!

Elsa and Anna are on their way to a day of birthday fun. Draw lines to show where the missing pieces of this picture should go.

Great job!

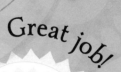

Draw a Snowgie

Draw your own snowgie by copying this one into the empty grid below, square by square. Then color it in!

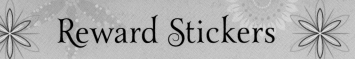

© Disney

© Disney

© Disney

© Disney

Just for Fun

Create a Cake

Anna's cake is so pretty!
What kind of cake would you like
at your birthday party? Draw it here.

Anna

Anna

Anna

Anna

Anna

Looks yummy!

A Touch of Fever

Poor Elsa has a fever, so Anna is taking care
of her sick big sister. Can you spot six things that
are missing from the picture on the opposite page?

Draw the missing items, and then color the picture.

Beautiful coloring!

19

Answers on page 31

Little Lost Brother

One of the snowgies is lost! Help him find his way through the maze to his big brother Olaf.

Start →

Finish

Good job!

20

Answer on page 32

Anna's Perfect Day

Elsa wants everything to be perfect for Anna's big day!
Read all about it below. Draw a line between each
picture and the place it belongs in the story.

Elsa wakes up Anna and gives her a pretty new ☐ .

Anna has to follow a string to find all of her ☐ .

Elsa and Anna ride a ☐ down the stairs! At the end

of the day, Anna meets all of her friends in the courtyard,

and Sven uses his antlers to cut the birthday ☐ .

dress   presents   cake   bicycle

Well done!

Present Puzzle

Help Kristoff arrange all of Anna's presents. There should be one of each present in each row and column. Write the correct letter in each empty square to complete the puzzle.

Perfect!

Answer on page 32

Olaf's Big Day

Olaf is imagining his own perfect birthday party. What do you think it would look like? Draw it here, and then color Olaf in.

Super drawing!

© Disney

Special Friends

Kristoff and Sven want to make Anna's birthday extra special. Look carefully at these two pictures. Can you spot six differences in the picture on the right?

Color a flower for each
difference you find.

Did you find them all?

25

Answer on page 32

Shadow Match

Olaf is having fun chasing his shadow in the snow. Find the one that matches him perfectly.

A

B

C

D

E

Great!

Add your reward sticker here.

Answer on page 32

To the Ice Palace

Olaf's little brothers are going to live with Marshmallow in the Ice Palace. Help Kristoff, Sven, and Olaf find the right path to get them there.

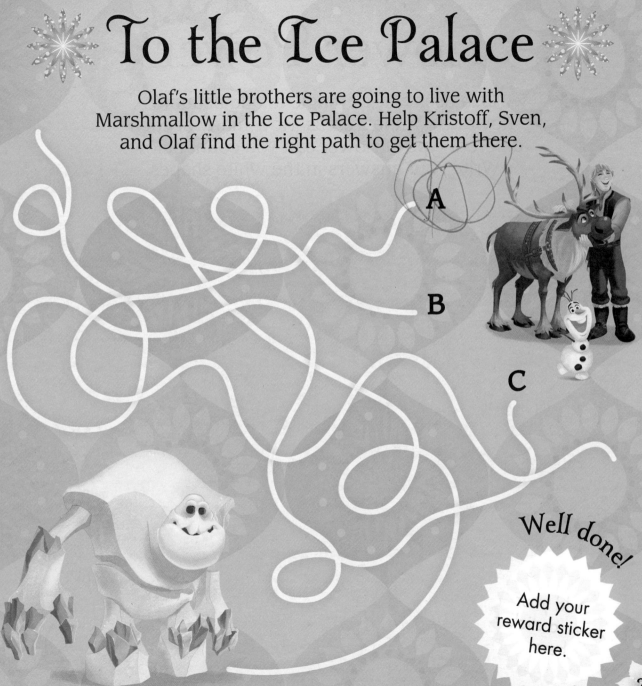

A

B

C

Well done!

Add your reward sticker here.

Answer on page 32

Flower Power

Elsa uses her ice magic to add beautiful flowers to Anna's dress. How many of each different type of flower can you count below? Write your answers in the white shapes.

Well done!

28

4   5   2   3

Summer Search

Olaf just loves summer! How many times can you find the word "summer" in the grid below? Look up, down, across, and diagonally.

```
s u m m e r s u
s u e m r m u r
r e m r m s m e
s e r m u e m m
r m e r e m e m
s u m m e r r u
m u r e m m u s
```

Fantastic!

Answer on page 32

Sisterly Love

Anna is so happy that she can care for her big sister. It's the best present of all! How many snowgies can you see hiding in the picture below?

There are __ snowgies

Great searching!

Answer on page 32

Answers

Page 2
There are 11 snowgies.

Page 3
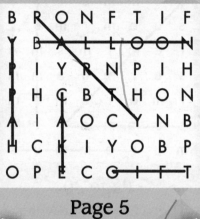

Page 5

Page 6
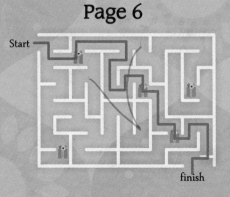

Page 6
Anna will collect three presents.

Page 7
There are six sunflowers.

Page 9

Page 10
Line C.

Page 11
Snowgie B is different.

Page 14
Cake E doesn't have a match.

Page 15

Page 19

Answers

Page 20

Start →

Finish

Page 21

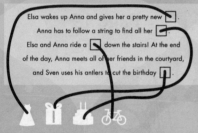

Elsa wakes up Anna and gives her a pretty new 👗.
Anna has to follow a string to find all her 🎁.
Elsa and Anna ride a 🚲 down the stairs! At the end
of the day, Anna meets all of her friends in the courtyard,
and Sven uses his antlers to cut the birthday 🎂.

Page 22

			C
B	C		
		D	
	D		B

Pages 24–25

Page 26

Shadow D is the
correct match.

Page 27

Line A.

Page 28

4   5   2   3

Page 29

The word "summer"
appears six times.

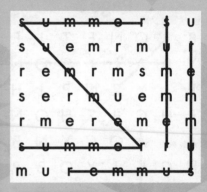

Page 30

There are 10 snowgies.